MW01461487

To:

_____

From:

_____

♥ Message: ♥

_____

_____

_____

A Kite Like Me
ISBN: 979-8-9913365-0-5
© 2024 by Sandi Brown and Dr. Michelle Caulk
Illustrations © 2024 Phil A. Smouse
All rights reserved worldwide.

Published by Gateway Creative Broadcasting, Inc.
13358 Manchester Road, Suite 100, St. Louis, MO 63131

Published in association with DeMoss Publishing Group, LLC.

Unless otherwise noted, all Scripture references are taken from the Holy Bible, New International Version®, NIV®, © 1973, 1978, 1984, 2011 Biblica, Inc.® Used by permission of Zondervan. All rights reserved worldwide. www.zondervan.com. The "NIV" and "New International Version" are trademarks registered in the United States Patent and Trademark Office by Biblica, Inc.®

No part of this publication may be reproduced, stored in a retrieval system, or transmitted in any form or by any means electronic, mechanical, photocopy, recording, scanning, or other— except for brief quotations in critical reviews or articles, without the prior written permission of the publisher.

Cover design by Phil A. Smouse

Printed in South Korea
First printing 2024

BOOKS BY SANDI BROWN
Choose Joy
A Little More Peace
Findable Joy

BOOKS BY SANDI BROWN AND DR. MICHELLE CAULK
Healing Out Loud

Visit https://www.joyfmonline.org/

A Kite Like Me

Finding God's Freedom in Wounded Places

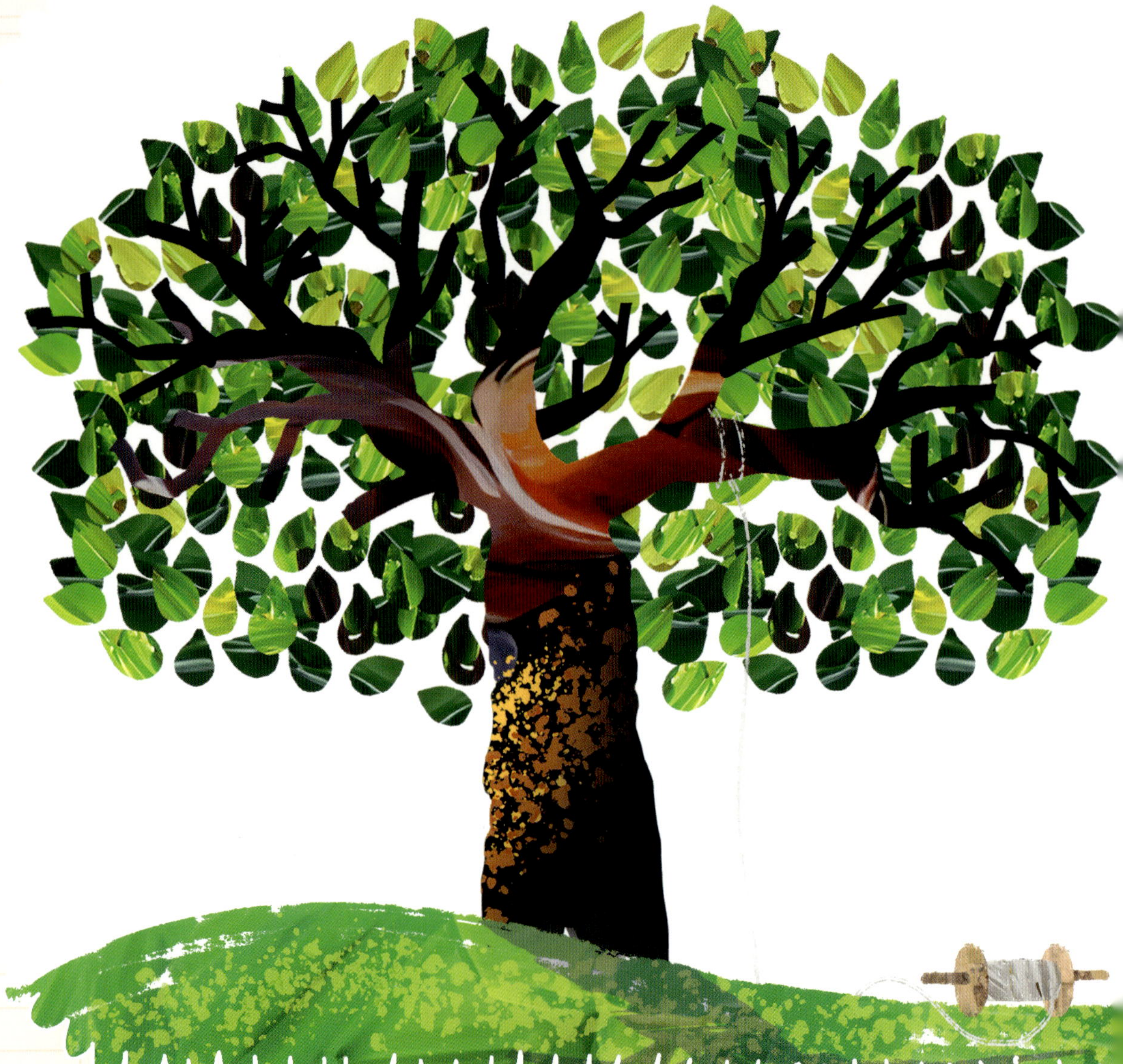

Before we Begin...

I began to write this story when I was sixteen, after going through some "heart bruising" experiences. To process my feelings, I put pen to paper. Even though no one ever read my private journaling, the exercise served a purpose for me. It was the first time any of my inner stuff made its way out, in any form. But once on paper, my reflections sat. For decades. In fact, I forgot about those pages until I was in counseling with Dr. Michelle Caulk.

I dug my notebook out of storage and, while reading it to Michelle, we realized the beauty and power in healing out loud. We also knew that there was now more of the story to write. Much more. So, after our counseling relationship ended, we did.

Our hope is that this story resonates with you and reminds you of the future and freedom God is authoring for you.

Sandi and Michelle

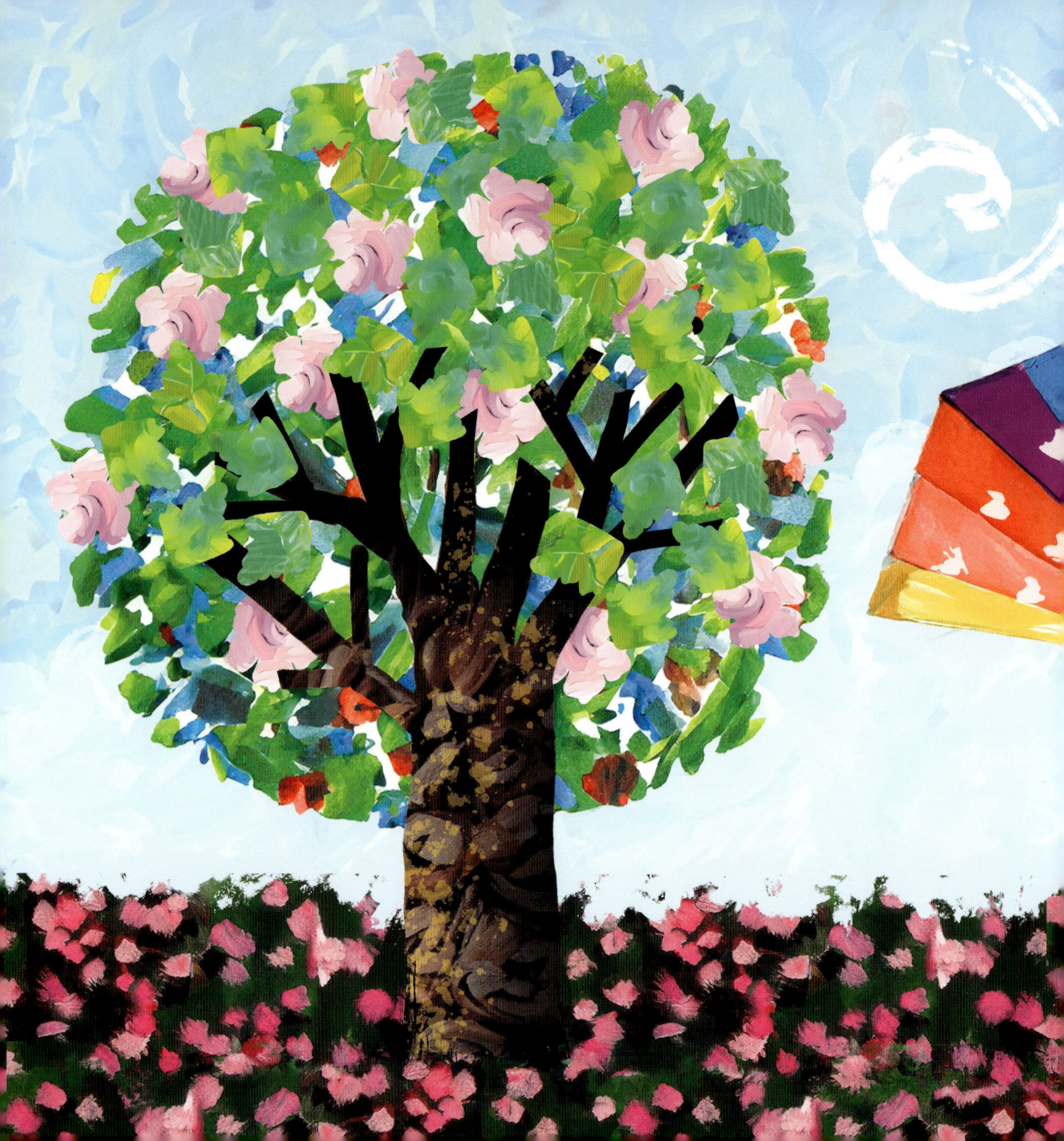

There once was a kite that loved to fly.
She felt beautiful. Colorful. And free.
She felt known by the Breeze and
completely alive in the sky.

She was a kite like me.

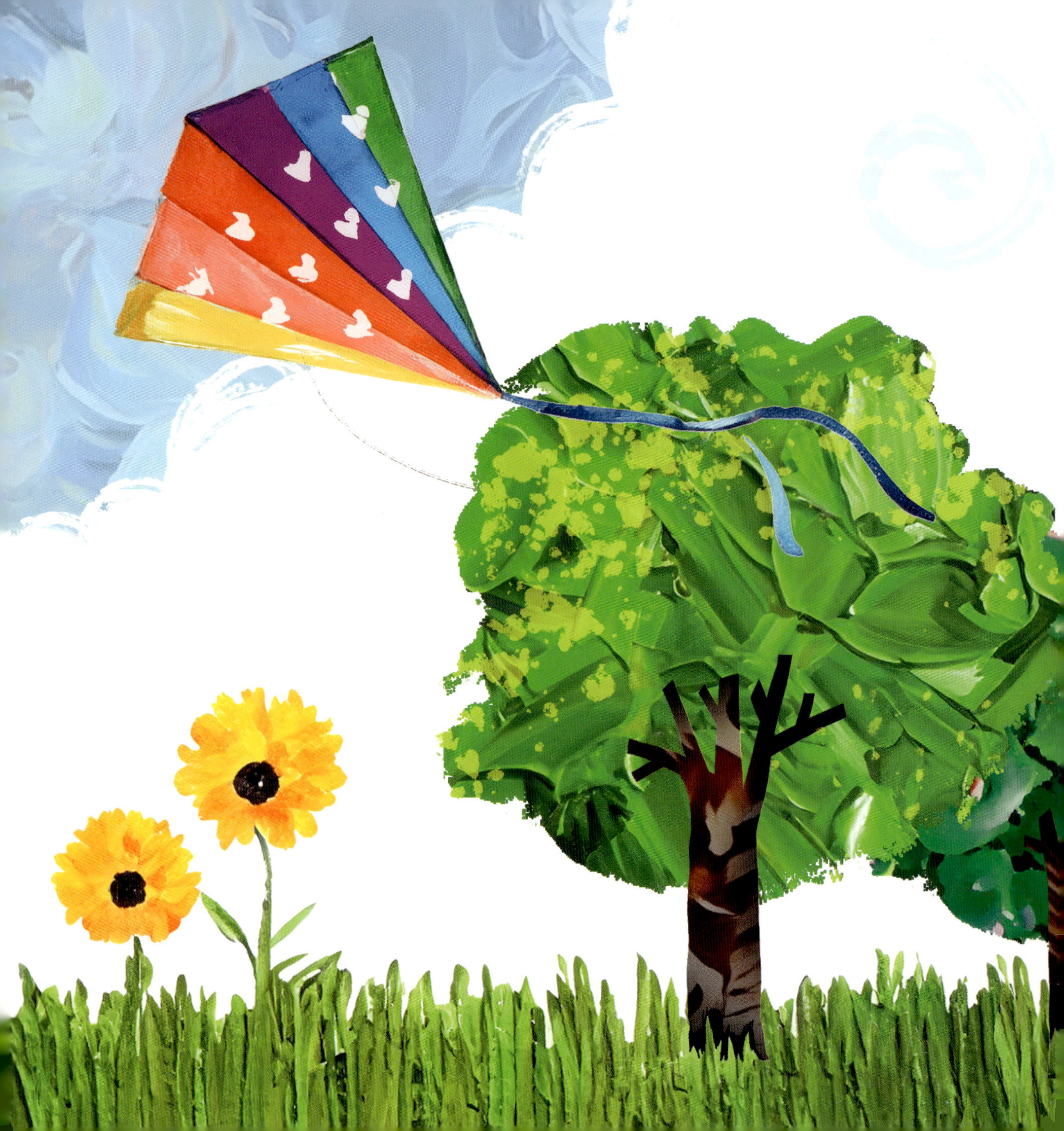

One day, the young kite was flying while her dad watched below. He held her string loosely in his hand. She was thankful that he was holding onto her.

She danced around the trees and smiled.
But her dad looked distracted.
He looked away.

He let go of her string. It was goodbye.

Goodbye...

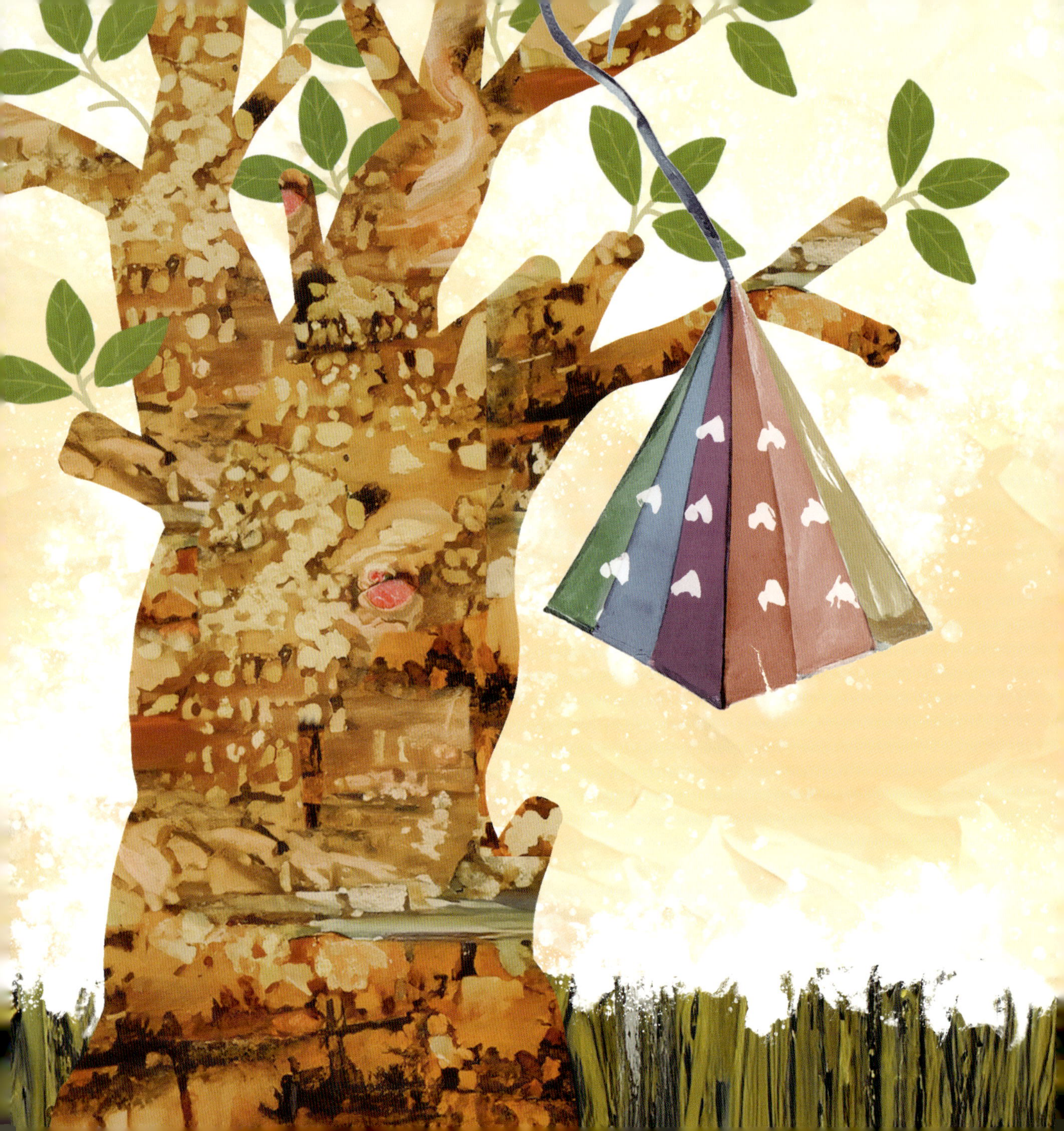

The kite felt alone, confused and sad.
She rested on a tree branch
and began to cry.

"Why did he leave? Was it my fault?
I guess I'm not a good enough kite."
She felt less beautiful. Less colorful.
Less free to dance.

She was a kite like me.

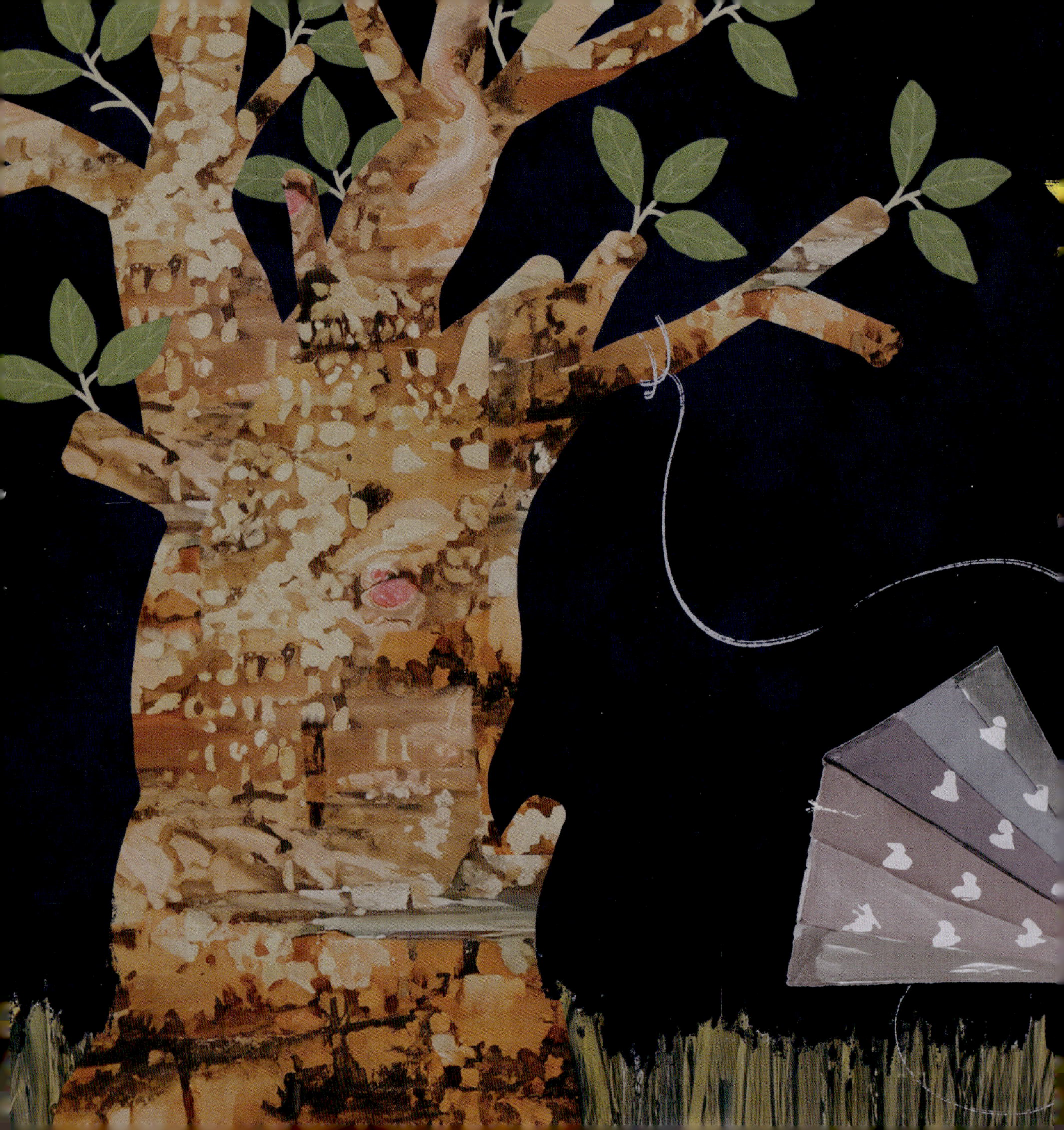

One day, without warning, the kite felt a tug. She looked down and noticed someone clutching her string.

A man grimaced up at her as he tugged and tugged. The kite fought as best as she could, but he was just too strong.

She crashed to the ground.
A few more tears appeared
in her fabric as she quietly wept.
"Why did he hurt me? Was it my fault?"

She felt broken.
Like she lost a lot.

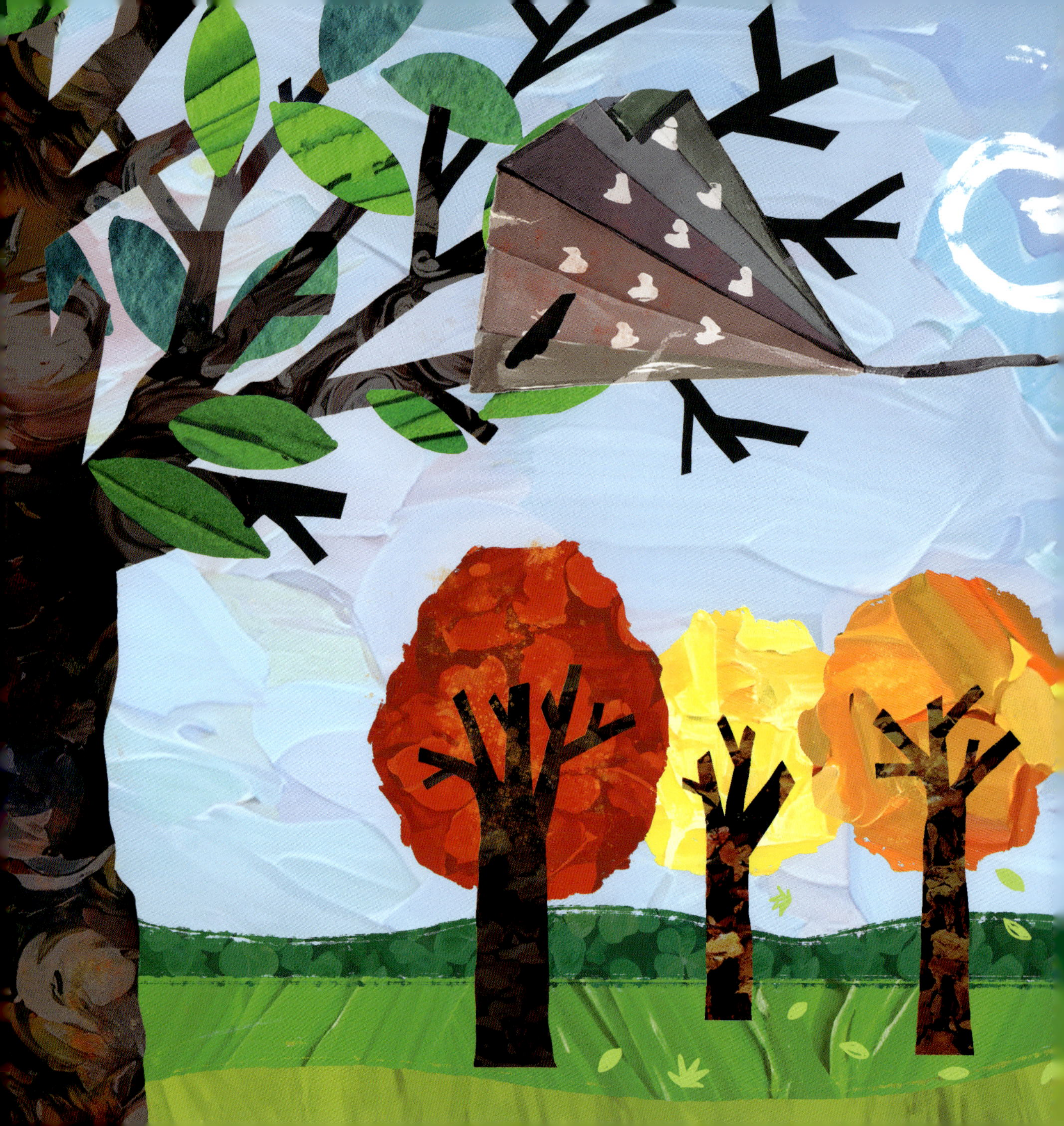

The kite didn't want to fly anymore.

Her fabric felt too fragile, too tattered
and torn. She didn't feel beautiful.
So, she spent more time in the branches
than she did in the sky.

It wasn't where she was meant to be,
but it felt like a safe place. A familiar place.
But the Breeze was close. Calling. Inviting.
Reminding her that she was made to fly.

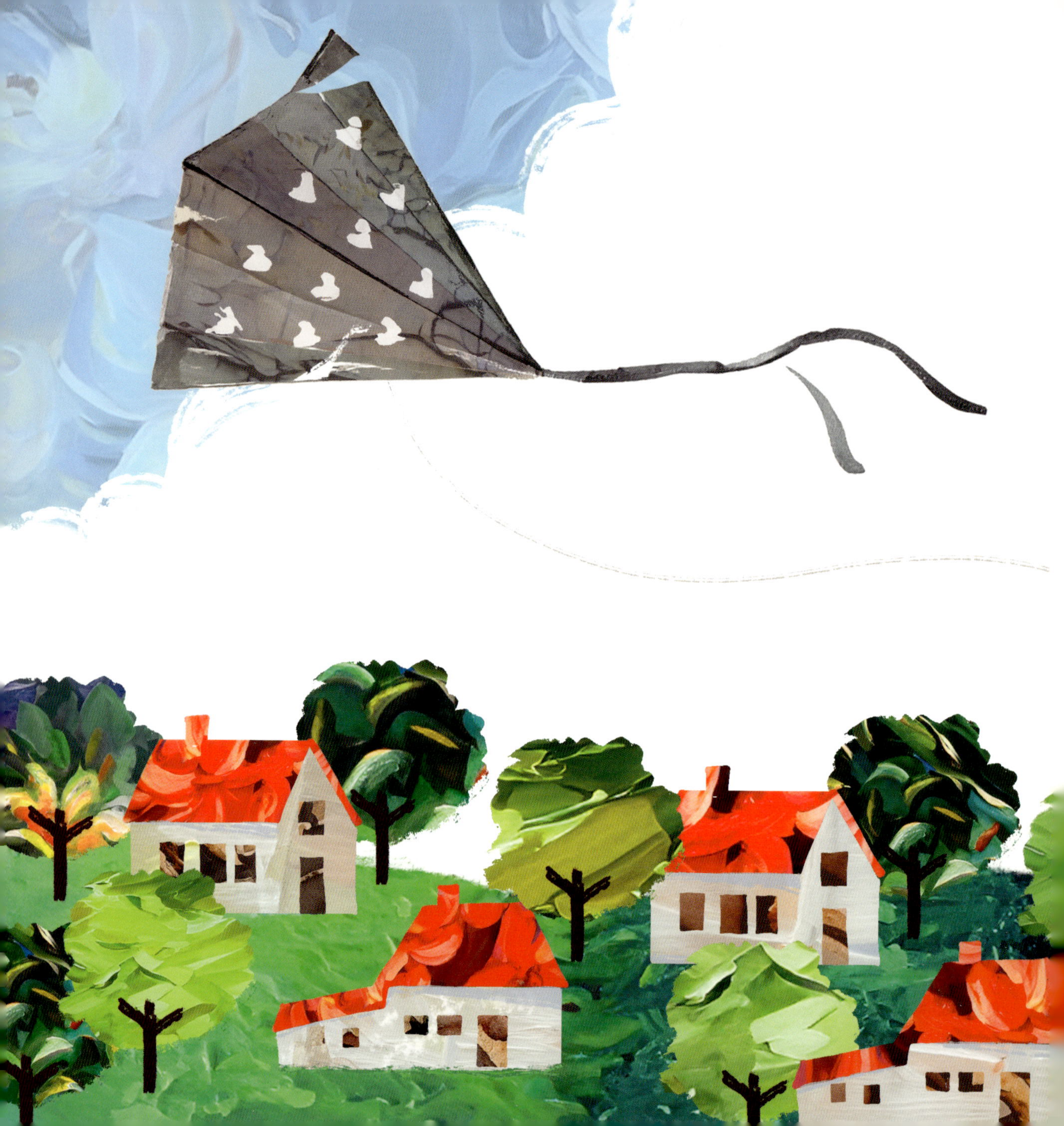

Its invitation was tender. And kind.

She cautiously leaned into the wind
but flying was different now.
Her string was a little longer.
She felt a little safer that way.

"If no one can see me, no one
can hurt me," she thought.

She was a kite like me.

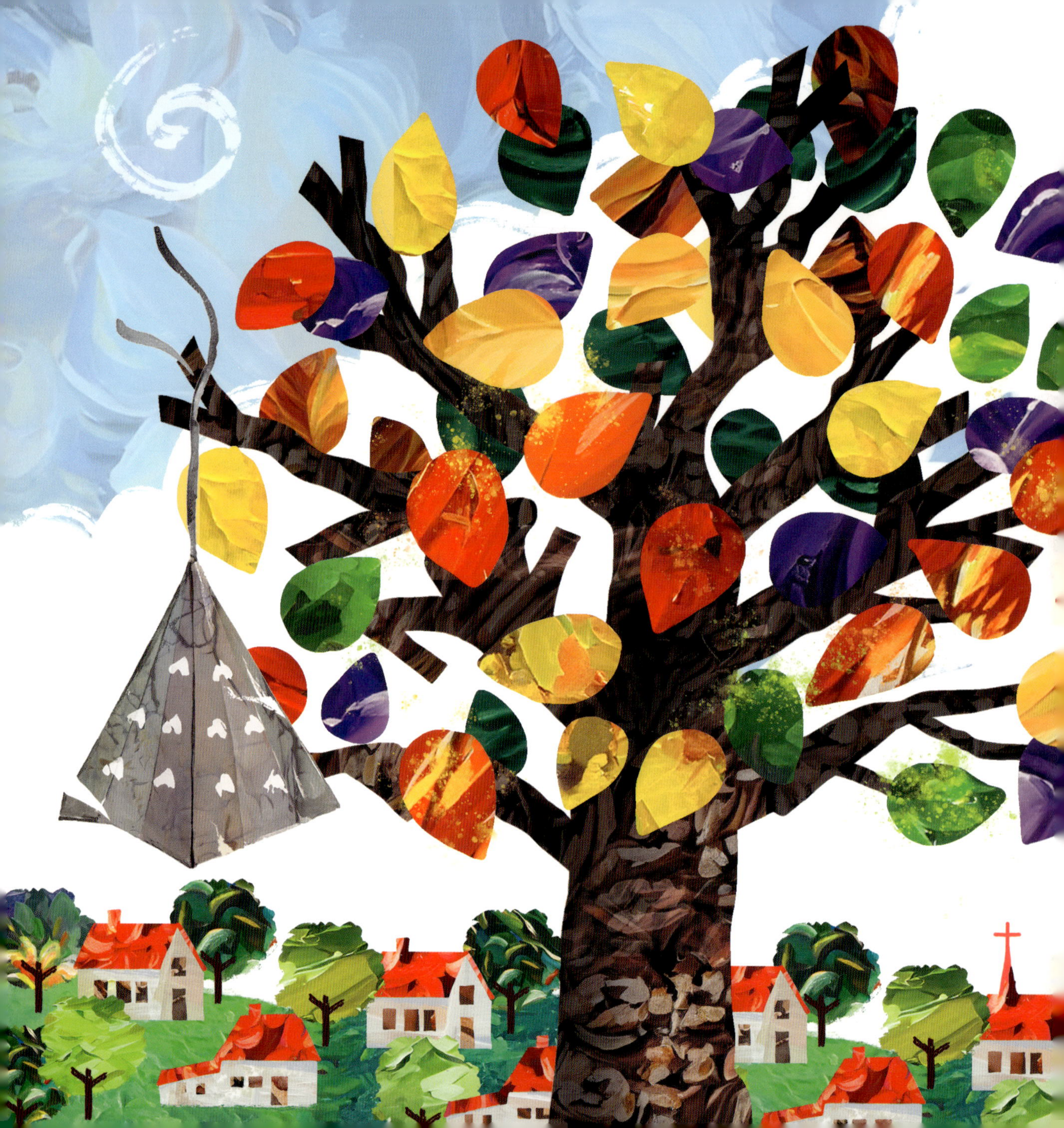

Many days later, the kite realized
that something was wrong.
She could still feel the Breeze.
She could still see the sky above
and the ground below.

But that was the problem—

she saw the same piece of sky
and the same piece of ground.
She wasn't flying. She was stuck.
Tangled in the tree branches.

How long had she been stuck in the same place?
She didn't know.

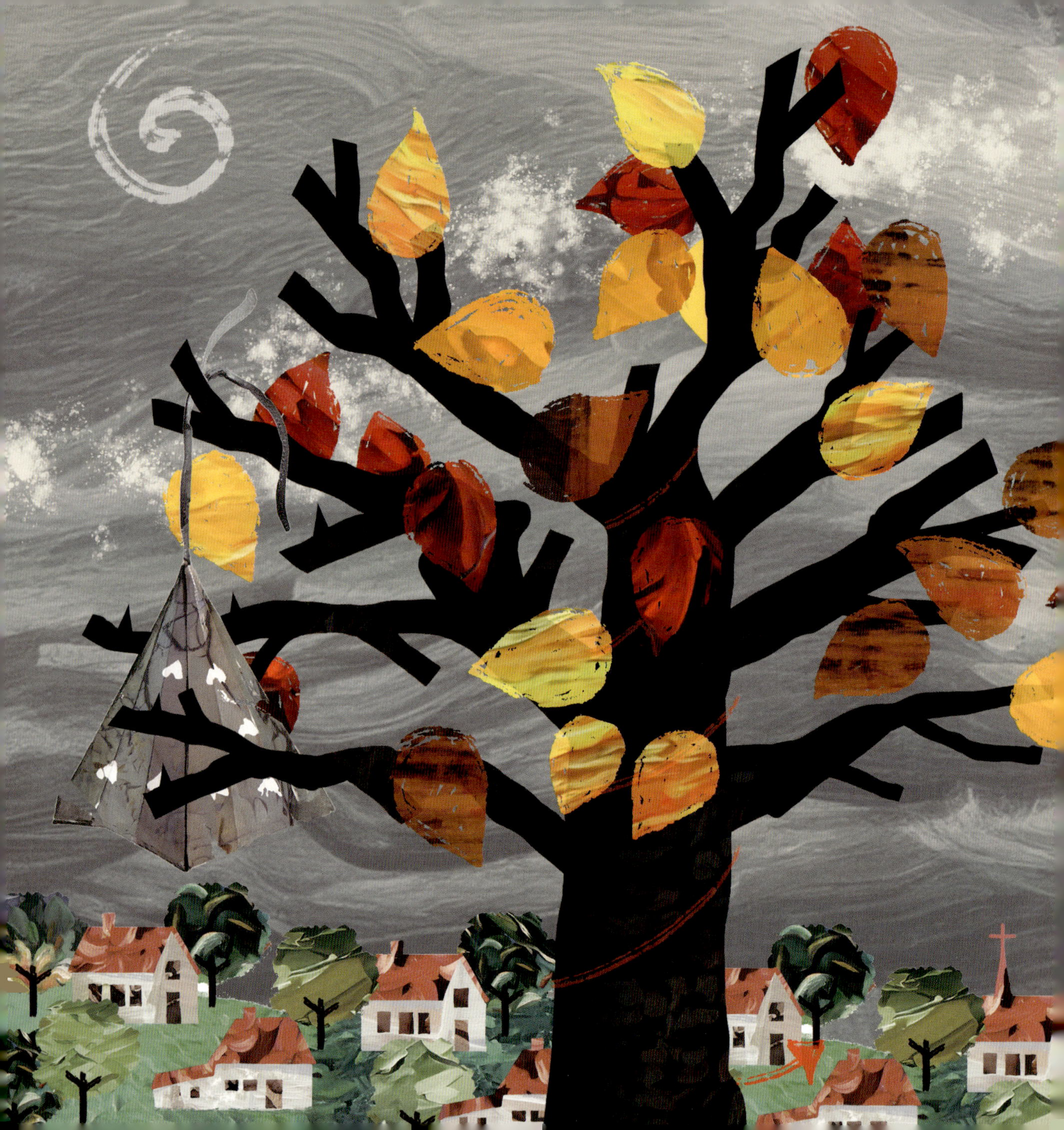

The kite tried to get free on her own.
But the more she struggled, the more tangled she got. The tree branches were strong and thorny, firmly wrapped around her string.

And the tree was **LOUD!**

The tree told her to stay right where she was because she wasn't beautiful. Or colorful.
She could never be free.

The tree's shouts were oh so convincing.
She believed every word.

She was a kite like me.

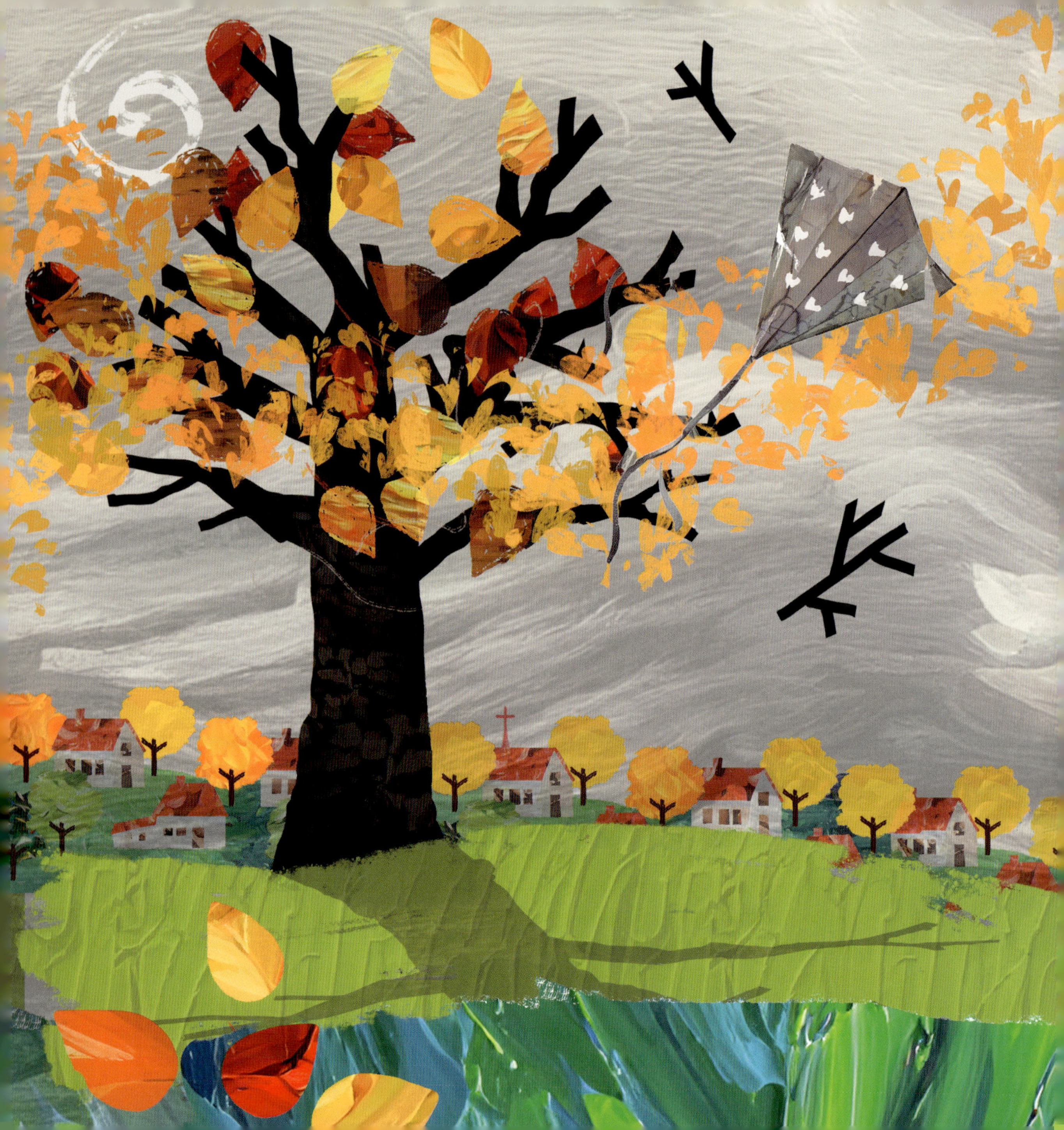

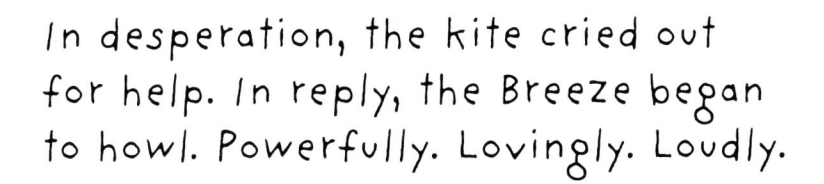

In desperation, the kite cried out for help. In reply, the Breeze began to howl. Powerfully. Lovingly. Loudly.

It felt unsettling, like the kite was losing her grip. But isn't that what she wanted?

The wind picked up and with each untangled string came a new sense of release: Shame. Rejection. Pain.

One by one the knots and tangles were exposed. Freed. With each gust of the Breeze, another stubborn tree limb let go of the kite. Or was she letting go? Either way, freedom was coming.

Piece by piece. Peace.

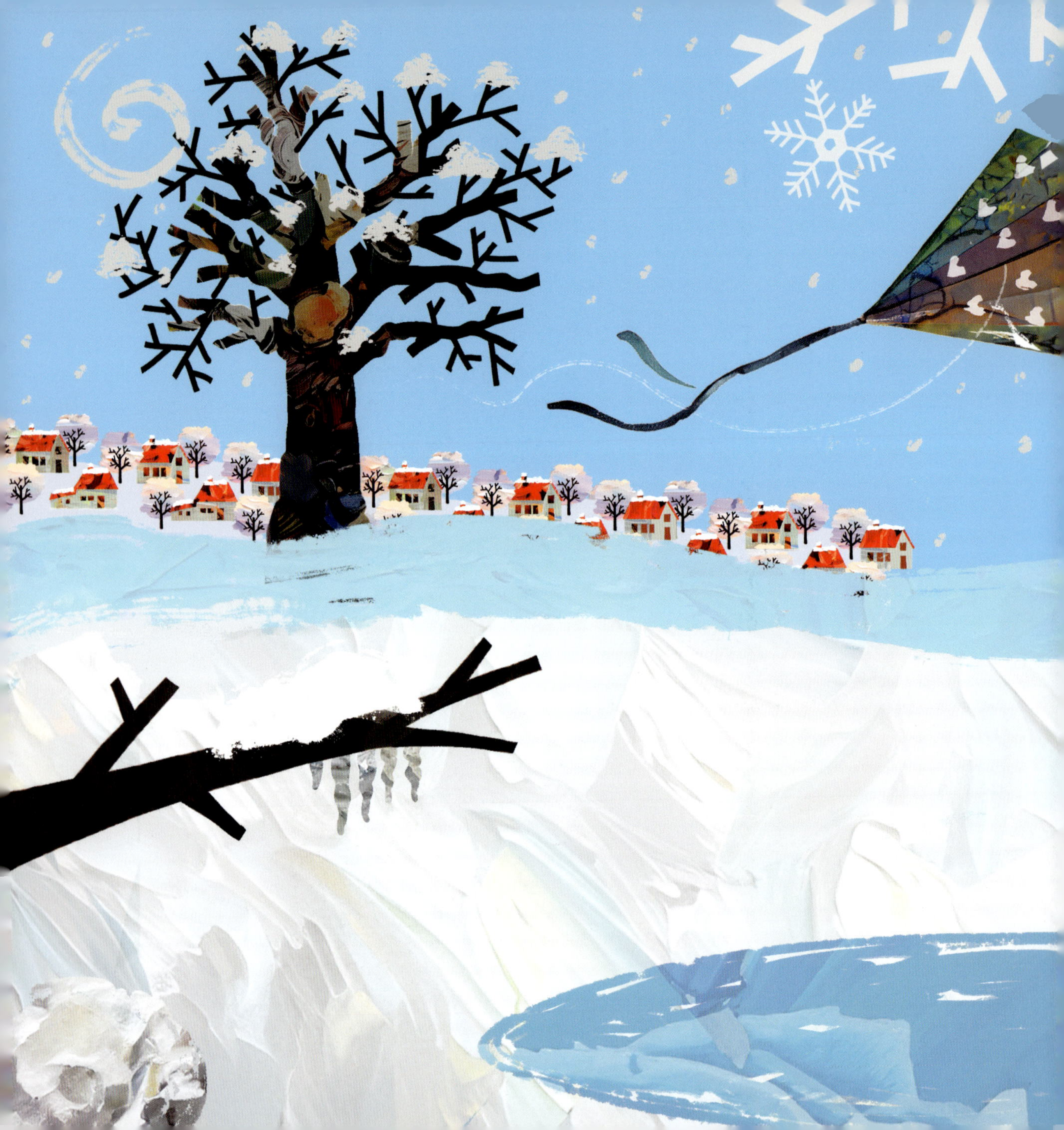

The Breeze called out to the kite with
an invitation to trust...to fly again.
The kite felt conflicted. She wanted to fly.
To experience newfound freedom.
To dance unhindered by the branches
of the familiar tree.

But deep down there was a lingering doubt.
She whispered it into the Breeze.

"Can broken kites still fly?"

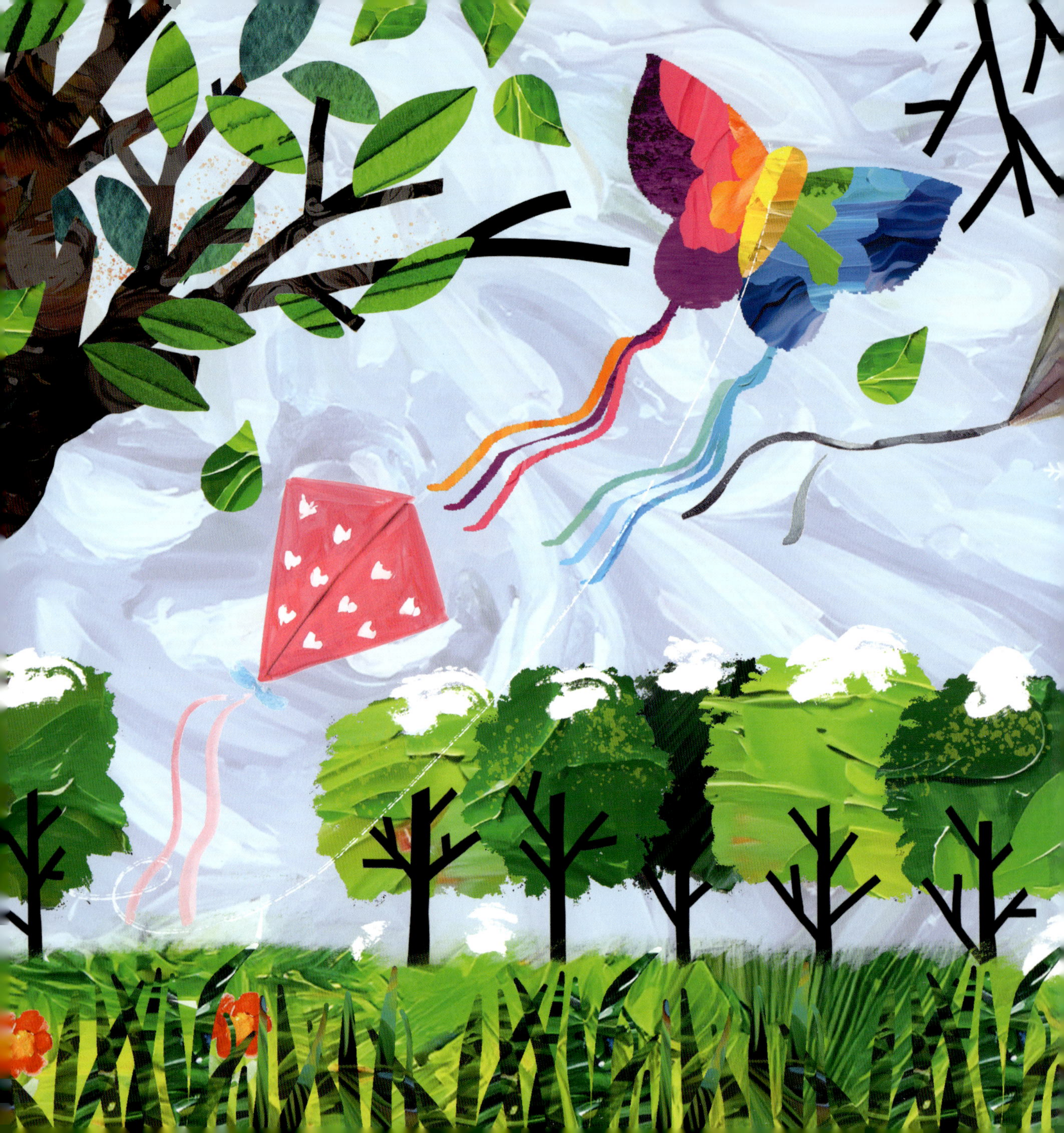

"We can!" exclaimed a nearby kite.

She flew in close and said,
"Because, friend, you are not broken.
Can't you see?

You are wounded, tattered and torn.
But the Breeze has set you free.
To heal. To smile. To dance."

"You see, you are a kite like me."

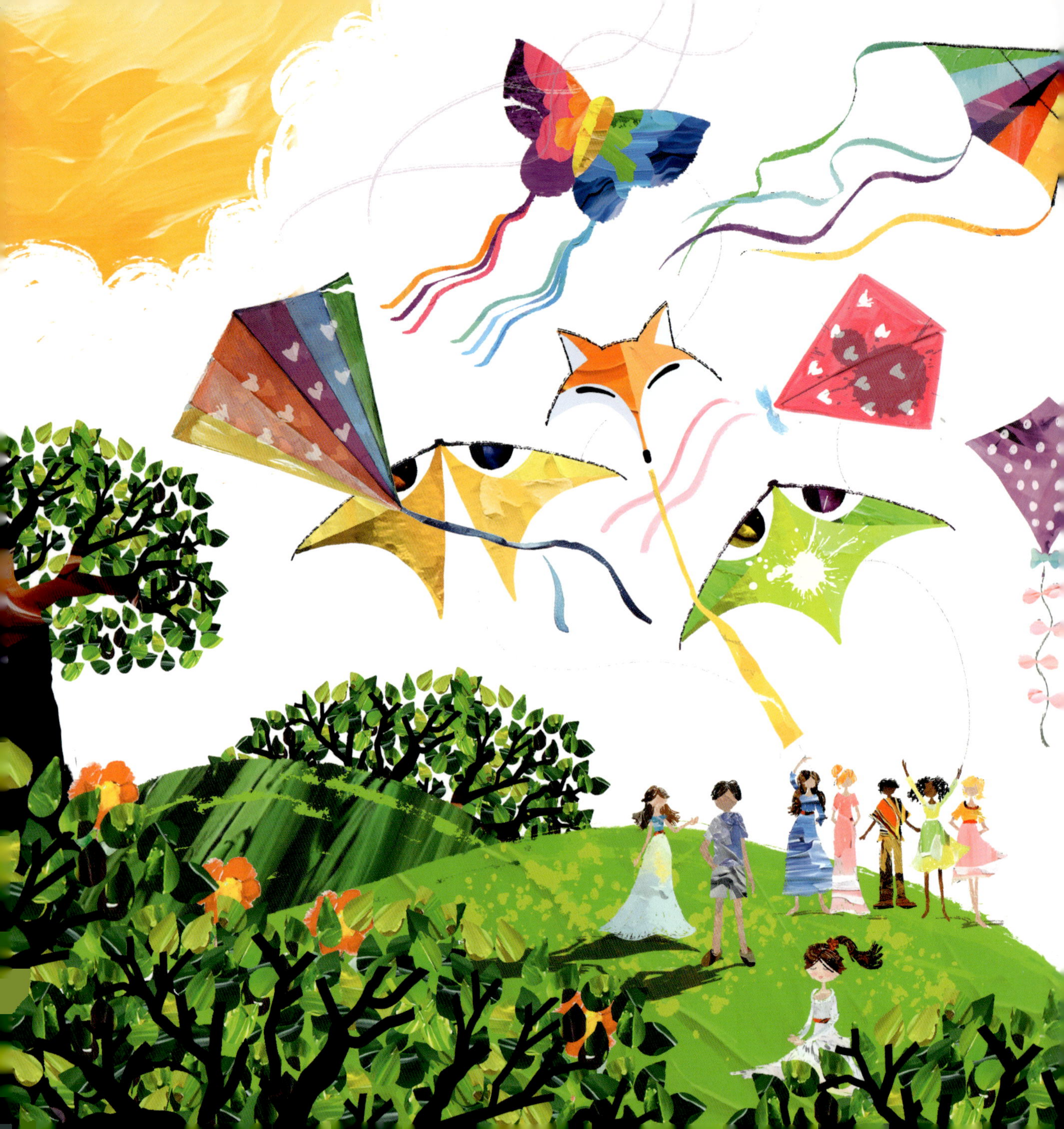

That's when the kite could see.

Hundreds of other kites dancing in the sky. Tattered. Torn. Faded in places. Yet beautiful. Colorful. Free.

She could hear them singing encouragement to her: "Come fly with us! It's who you were made to be!"

The kite took a deep breath, closed her eyes and jumped into the sky.

At first, freedom felt unfamiliar and awkward. How long had it been since she felt truly free? Or beautiful?

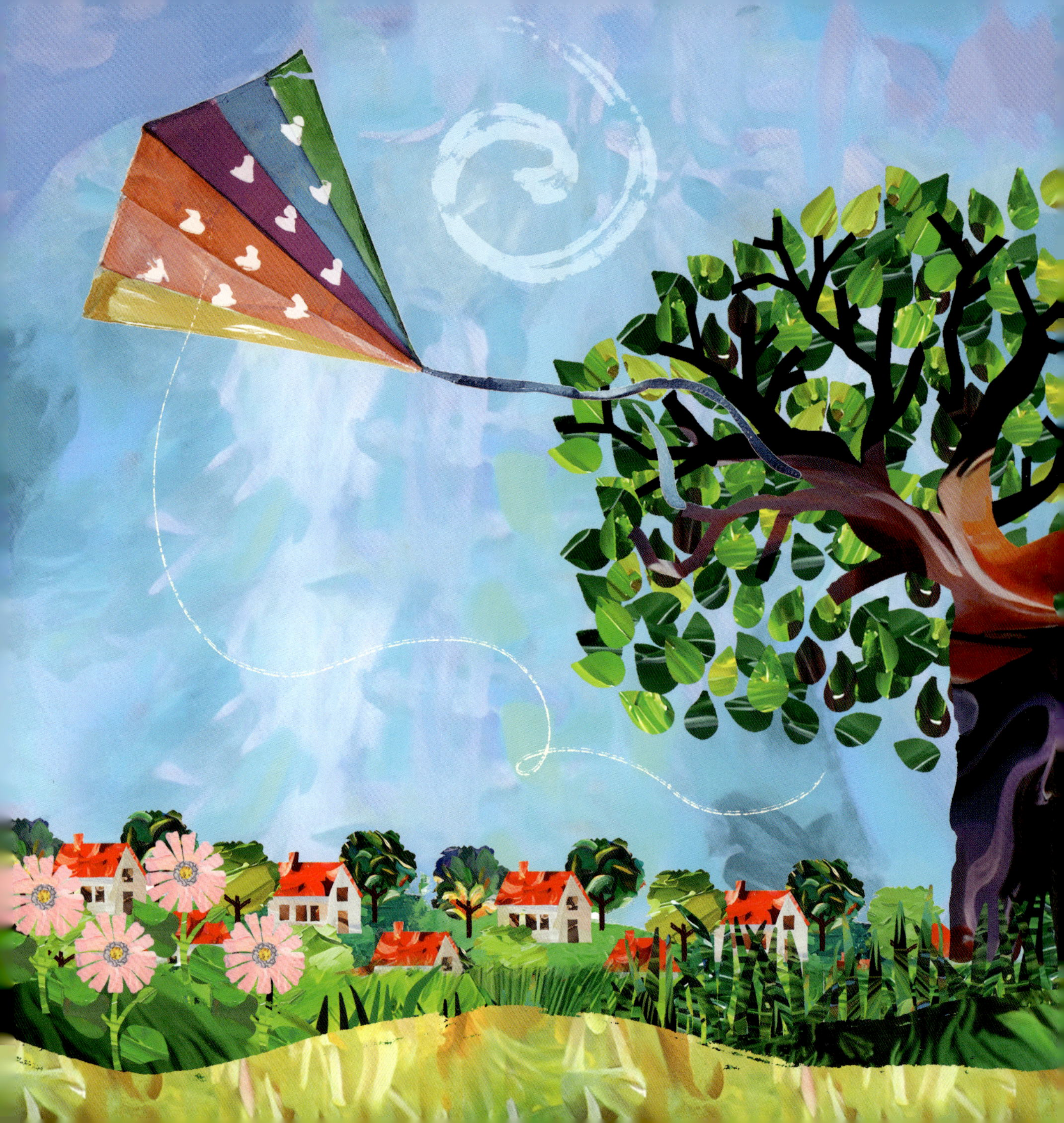

A gust of hope caught her.
Embraced her.

She was still tattered, torn
and faded. But the Breeze
loved her anyway.

She came alive!
She was free to heal
and dance. Playfully dipping
and twirling across the sky.

The wind was her song.

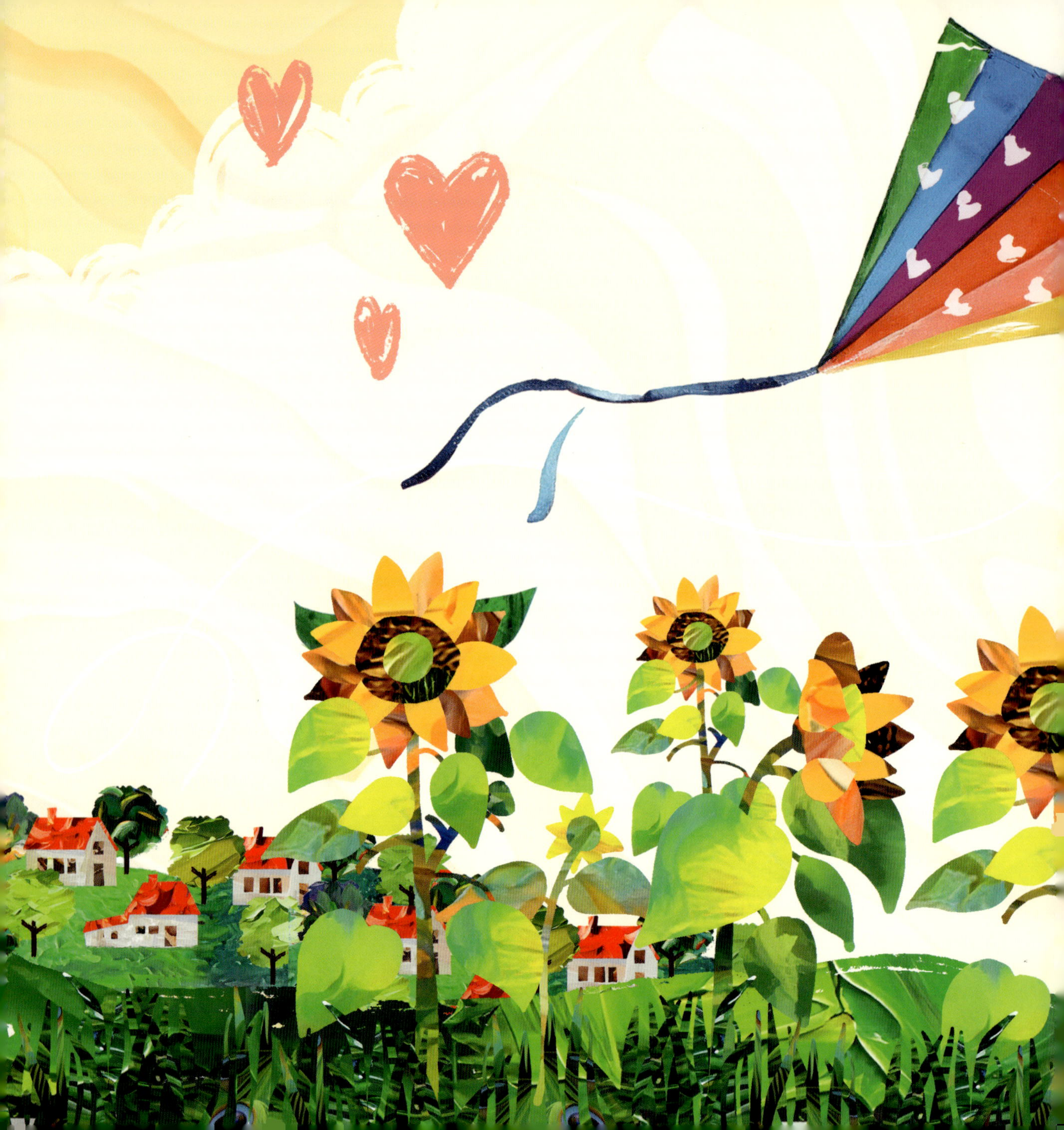

Occasionally, the kite still heard the
branches calling out to her. But the voice
of the Breeze was faithfully calling as well.
It sounded like hope. Like home.
And its voice was now oh so familiar.

Day after day, the kite soared in the sky.
The Breeze was healing her torn places.
It was inviting her into new places.
Trust. Love. Joy. It was the life she always
longed for. What she was made for.

She sang a new song of freedom.
She sang it loud enough so
that other tangled kites in
the familiar tree could hear.

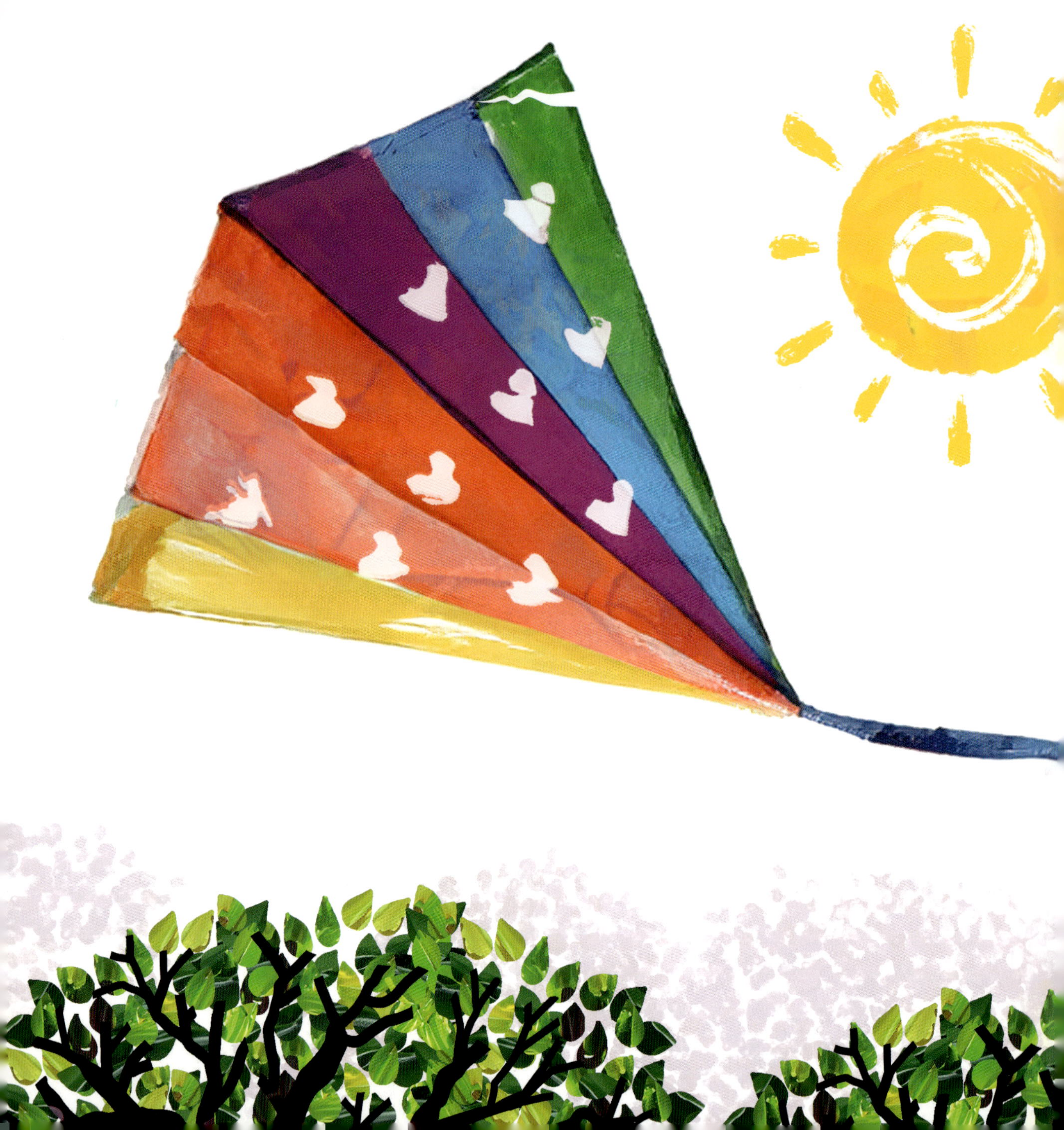

Tattered. Healing. And free.
The beautiful kite danced.

She is a kite like me.

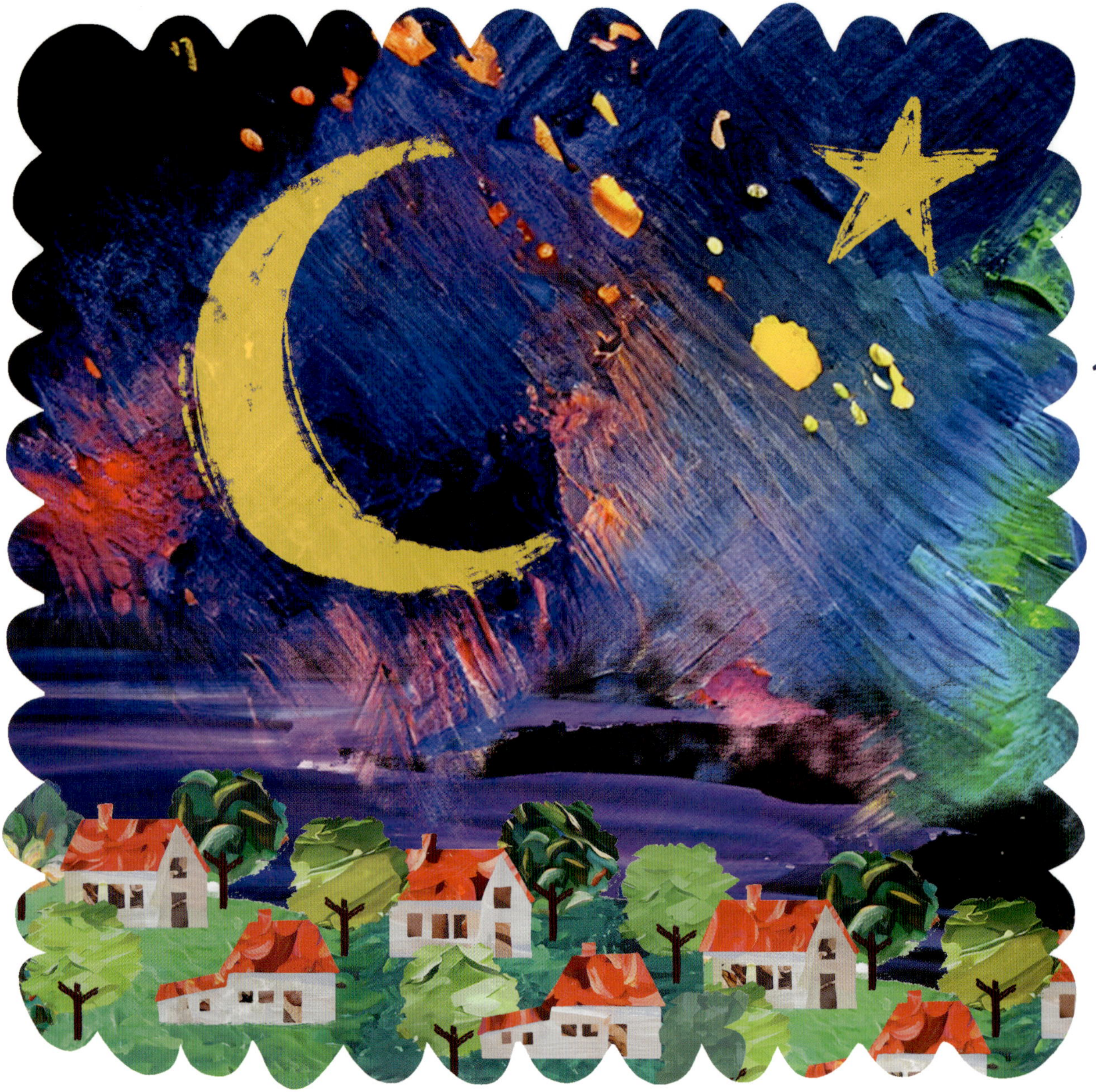

"He brought me out into a spacious place; he rescued me because he delighted in me."

Psalm 18:19

A Moment to Reflect and Share

Your story began before you were even aware, and it is still unfolding. Have you ever considered who you were created to be? What good and not so good things have shaped you?

What emotions of the kite do you connect with? What may be the root for some of those feelings or insecurities?

Have you lost someone important in your life—through divorce, death, or rejection? God promises to be close when your heart is breaking. He can bring comfort and peace into your grief and loss.

How we feel about ourselves does not always match up with how God sees us. Have you ever felt less beautiful, unlovable or broken? How does that bump up against the fact that God delights in you?

You may hear different messages—like the tree, other kites, and the Breeze. Which voice(s) do you listen to the most? How do their words affect you?

Who do you talk to when you're struggling? Is there anything you're feeling prompted to share with them? Is God inviting you to encourage someone who may need a friend?

Can you relate to feeling stuck? What would healing look like in your life? Is there a "next step" that God is inviting you to take?

The Promises of God

Psalm 34:18
"The Lord is close to the brokenhearted and saves those who are crushed in spirit."

Romans 8:39
"Neither height nor depth, nor anything else in all creation, will be able to separate us from the love of God that is in Christ Jesus our Lord."

Jeremiah 29:11
"'For I know the plans I have for you,' declares the Lord, 'plans to prosper you and not to harm you, plans to give you hope and a future.'"

John 8:36
"So if the Son sets you free, you will be free indeed."

Psalm 139:13-14
"For you created my inmost being; you knit me together in my mother's womb. I praise you because I am fearfully and wonderfully made; your works are wonderful, I know that full well."

About the Authors

Sandi Brown is the founder and President of Gateway Creative Broadcasting in St. Louis, MO. where she leads two radio stations, JOY FM and BOOST RADIO. Sandi previously worked as a Creative Writer and Producer for Focus on the Family. Sandi is co-host of the JOY FM Morning Show and has written four books. She loves to spend time with her family, go on walks and laugh, or "cackle" as her friends and co-workers call it.

Dr. Michelle Caulk is a licensed counselor and counselor educator. She founded a counseling center, Hope Narrative Mental Health Services, and joyfully helps clients live in hope and purpose. Michelle is currently an Assistant Professor and the Director of Clinical Experiences at Huntington University. Sandi and Michelle's first book, *Healing Out Loud: How to Embrace God's Love When You Don't Like Yourself*, gives an inside view of therapy and healing from both sides of the couch.

Phil A. Smouse wanted to be a scientist. But scientists don't get wonderful cards and letters from friends like you, so he decided to draw and color instead. You can learn more about his award winning picture books at www.philsmouse.com.